Put Beginning Readers on the Right Track with
ALL ABOARD READING™

The All Aboard Reading series is especially for beginning readers. Written by noted authors and illustrated in full color, these are books that children really and truly *want* to read—books to excite their imagination, tickle their funny bone, expand their interests, and support their feelings. With four different reading levels, All Aboard Reading lets you choose which books are most appropriate for your children and their growing abilities.

Picture Readers—for Ages 3 to 6
Picture Readers have super-simple texts with many nouns appearing as rebus pictures. At the end of each book are 24 flash cards—on one side is the rebus picture; on the other side is the written-out word.

Level 1—for Preschool through First Grade Children
Level 1 books have very few lines per page, very large type, easy words, lots of repetition, and pictures with visual "cues" to help children figure out the words on the page.

Level 2—for First Grade to Third Grade Children
Level 2 books are printed in slightly smaller type than Level 1 books. The stories are more complex, but there is still lots of repetition in the text and many pictures. The sentences are quite simple and are broken up into short lines to make reading easier.

Level 3—for Second Grade through Third Grade Children
Level 3 books have considerably longer texts, use harder words and more complicated sentences.

All Aboard for happy reading!

Photo credits: pp. 11, 13, and 14, Neg. Nos. K17360, 5789, 2A5378, and 314438, Courtesy Dept. of Library Services, American Museum of Natural History.

ISBN 0-448-41575-5 A B C D E F G H I J

Level 3
Grades 2-3

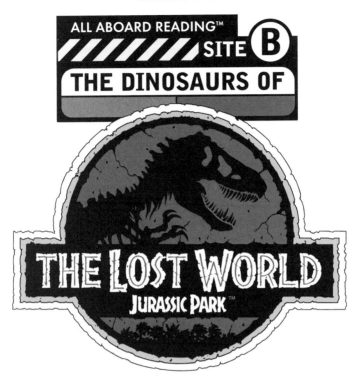

THE DINOSAURS OF THE LOST WORLD: JURASSIC PARK

By Jennifer Dussling

**With photos from the movie
THE LOST WORLD: *JURASSIC PARK*
and *JURASSIC PARK***

Grosset & Dunlap • New York

Lost World!

On the island Isla Sorna, by the edge of a dense jungle, Nick van Owen and Sarah Harding race into a trailer. Nick is carrying something in his arms. It is a baby.

But this baby is not a human baby. It is the baby of one of the largest, most feared killers ever to walk the earth. It is the baby of a Tyrannosaurus rex.

Inside the trailer, Ian Malcolm, Sarah, and Nick make a cast for the baby rex. Its leg is broken. And a baby dinosaur cannot live in the wild with a broken leg. There are too many dangers.

The baby rex does not know they are helping it. It screeches in pain.

From out of the jungle comes an answering roar. It is the roar of another tyrannosaur—a huge, 35-foot-tall T-rex. It is the baby's mother.

The mother rex knows her baby is hurt. She has come to protect it. She circles the trailer and tries to poke her giant head through the tiny window.

Then the huge tyrannosaur is joined by another rex. It is the baby's father.

Ian, Sarah, and Nick know there is not much time. They quickly finish the cast on the baby rex's broken leg. Then they push the little dinosaur out the trailer door.

The two huge tyrannosaurs sniff the baby. They make sure the baby is okay. Then all three disappear into the jungle.

Ian looks at Sarah. Sarah looks at Ian. They were very lucky. Nothing is more dangerous than an angry T-rex. Especially a T-rex who thinks its baby is in trouble. But the baby is fine. Hopefully the danger is over now.

Ian, Nick, and Sarah start to relax.

Then, all of a sudden, something smashes into the side of the trailer! It flips onto its side and everything goes flying—even Ian, Nick, and Sarah.

The tyrannosaurs are back!

Dinosaur Babies

Would a Tyrannosaurus rex really do this? Did T-rex mothers protect their babies? Did baby rexes cry for their mothers? We do not know for sure.

For over a hundred years, scientists have studied dinosaurs. We know a lot about them. We know how big they were. We know where they lived. We know which ones were hunters. And we know that baby dinosaurs hatched out of eggs.

But there are still many things we don't know. We don't know what color their skin really was. Or what sounds they made. Or how a mother dinosaur cared for her baby.

Not too long ago, people thought all dinosaurs were like most modern reptiles. They thought that, like a snake or lizard, a dinosaur mother laid her eggs and went away. Then the dinosaur babies took care of themselves. But people do not think this anymore. This view of dinosaurs has changed.

We now know some dinosaurs watched over their babies. They may have fed them. And protected them. And kept them warm. Some dinosaurs even sat on their eggs like a chicken.

A dinosaur laid several eggs at one time. Maiasauras laid their eggs in nests.

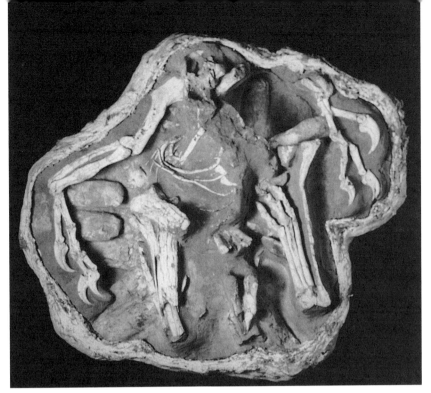

Scientists found this fossil of an Oviraptor sitting on its egg
in the Gobi Desert.

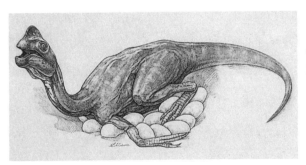

This drawing shows
how scientists think
the Oviraptor really
looked.

Other dinosaurs laid their eggs in a row.
And one dinosaur laid its eggs in two
matching rows. Scientists think this
dinosaur was a Troödon.

11

In the movie *Jurassic Park*, the dinosaurs were not supposed to hatch in the wild. Instead, the eggs were kept in a laboratory. Dr. Ellie Sattler and Dr. Alan Grant watched a baby dinosaur break out of its egg.

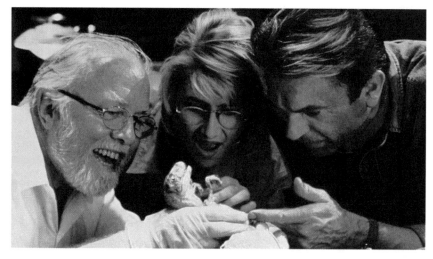

But four years later, in *The Lost World*: *Jurassic Park*, the dinosaurs run wild on Site B. The different dinosaurs—from the raptors to the tyrannosaurs—have made their own nesting grounds on the island. In each nesting ground, a different dinosaur lays its own type of egg.

Dinosaur eggs came in many shapes and sizes. Some were round. Some were football shaped. And some looked like big potatoes.

One dinosaur egg fossil next to a chicken's egg.

A large dinosaur egg could be the size of a melon—or even as big as a soccer ball. That is a big egg. It is much bigger than a chicken's egg. But think about how big a full-grown chicken is. Then think about how big a full-grown dinosaur was.

The biggest dinosaurs were over 100 feet long! Longer than a basketball court. Now the soccer ball egg does not seem so big.

A newly hatched baby dino would have been tiny next to its huge mother and father. But it probably grew very quickly.

Scientists have found thousands of dinosaur egg fossils. They do not even know which dinosaurs they all belong to!

This fossil shows six dinosaur eggs in a nest.

Still scientists have not found many
baby dinosaur fossils. These are very rare.

Is that because baby dinosaurs did
not die? No. Many babies did die. Their
lives were very dangerous. A little baby
dinosaur might be stepped on by a big
adult. Or it might be knocked over by
a big dinosaur's tail.

Some dinosaur
babies were pretty
helpless. They were
slower than the
grown-ups, and not
as strong. For a
meat-eating dinosaur,
like a Velociraptor,
a baby was probably
easier to catch and
kill than a full-grown
dinosaur.

So why haven't many baby dinosaur bones been found? Because a baby's bones were not as strong as a grown-up dinosaur's. Most of the time, a baby's bones turned into dirt before they could harden into stone fossils.

Still, from fossilized eggs and a few baby dinosaur fossils, scientists have learned much more about baby dinosaurs.

Some baby dinosaurs have been found with big dinosaurs nearby. Scientists think this means that some mother dinosaurs did watch over their babies. Maybe they brought the babies food. Maybe they attacked other dinosaurs who tried to hurt their babies—just like the Tyrannosaurus rex mother and father in *The Lost World: Jurassic Park*.

Scientists are trying to learn even more about baby dinosaurs.

Baby Stegosaurus

Ian, Nick, and Eddie Carr are looking for Sarah in the jungle. They know she is nearby. Then they hear a noise. Suddenly the trees behind them start to sway. Something big is walking through the jungle!

Everyone freezes. Then they see it. A Stegosaurus. No. A whole herd of stegosaurs. Grown-ups and babies!

Ian, Nick, and Eddie were lucky. On Isla Sorna there are scarier dinosaurs to run into. Stegosaurs were plant eaters— which means they did not hunt for meat. And their brains were only about the size of a golf ball.

Sarah was watching the stegos, too. She even got to pet a baby. It was gentle. But a grown Stegosaurus could also be very dangerous.

An adult Stegosaur had four sharp spikes on the end of its powerful tail. Plus it had two rows of hard plates along its back. Fully grown, it was the size of an elephant!

Stegosaurs laid big, oval eggs. When a baby hatched, it was pretty helpless. Baby stegosaurs did not have any tail spikes yet. They only had small back plates. These grew in as the baby got older.

Scientists have found grown-up and baby stegosaur fossils together. That's why they think stegosaurs may have lived in herds—as they do in *The Lost World*: *Jurassic Park*. Without big back plates and tail spikes, a baby stego needed grown-ups nearby to keep it safe.

Baby Triceratops

A grown-up Triceratops was a huge, powerful dinosaur. It weighed five tons and was as long as a school bus. Like the Stegosaurus, it was a plant eater. But that did not make Triceratops a wimp. Far from it. A Triceratops would have been a match for even a T-rex!

Three long, sharp horns stuck out from its head. They could be as long as golf clubs. And a hard neck frill—like a giant fan—covered its neck.

A baby Triceratops did not have these weapons, though. When it hatched, it had no horns and no neck frill. It was also probably pretty slow.

Baby Triceratops needed the grown-ups to protect them. So Triceratops may have lived in herds, too.

What would happen if a big hunter, like a T-rex, tried to get a baby trike? Scientists think the adult Triceratops may have stood in a circle around the babies. The three horns of each Triceratops would have faced out. Even a Tyrannosaurus rex would think twice before trying to get past that circle of sharp horns.

Baby Tyrannosaurus Rex

The Tyrannosaurus rex was one of the most ferocious hunters ever to walk the earth. Its teeth were as big as kitchen knives. And it had huge, powerful jaws.

But a baby tyrannosaur was not so scary. Like baby stegos and Triceratops, it was pretty helpless.

When it hatched, a baby tyrannosaur was probably the size of a cat. It could not keep up with a grown tyrannosaur. It could not get away from an enemy.

In *The Lost World*: *Jurassic Park*, Roland Tembo and Ajay Sidhu follow tracks to a cave. There they find a tyrannosaur nest. One baby is inside. It is waiting for its mother to bring it more food.

Some scientists even think a baby T-rex may have had feathers. Feathers! Why would a baby dinosaur have feathers?

Well, scientists think dinosaurs were a lot like birds. In fact, today's birds could be called a kind of dinosaur! In many ways, they are like meat-eating dinosaurs from millions of years ago.

Did a baby tyrannosaur really have downy feathers like a baby bird? Maybe. But no one knows for sure.

Is That All?

Were all baby dinosaurs helpless? No. The babies of small dinosaurs, like the Hypsilophodon and Compsognathus, probably were quick and nimble when they hatched. They had to be.

Why? Small dinosaurs did not fight big dinosaurs. Instead they usually ran away or hid. So parents could not protect a baby very well. The babies needed to be able to get away quickly, too.

In the past twenty years, many new and exciting discoveries about dinosaurs and their babies have been made. But there is still a lot more that we do not know. This, too, will change, though.

Scientists will dig up nests. They will find more eggs. Hopefully they will discover more baby dinosaur fossils.

And who knows? Maybe in the future, science will be able to bring dinosaurs back to life, just like in the movie *The Lost World*: *Jurassic Park*.

Glossary

Dinosaurs have very big names (even the little ones!). This list will help you know how to spell them—and say them.

Compsognathus (KOMP-sog-NAY-thus)
Hypsilophodon (hip-sih-LO-fuh-don)
Maiasaura (mah-ee-ah-SAW-ra)
Oviraptor (O-veh-RAP-tor)
Stegosaurus (STEG-uh-SAW-rus)
Triceratops (tri-SAIR-uh-tops)
Troödon (TROE-oh-don)
Tyrannosaurus rex
    (tye-RAN-uh-SAW-rus REX)
Velociraptor (vel-OSS-uh-RAP-tor)